DICK KING-SMITH

Hogsel and Gruntel

ILLUSTRATED BY
LIZ GRAHAM-YOOLL

Hogsel and Gruntel

Once upon a time there were two little piglets, brother and sister, called Hogsel and Gruntel. They were very unhappy, for their mother had died and their stepsow was not kind to them, so they ran away, into the forest.

They walked and walked, trotter in trotter, until they were exhausted and it seemed that they must die from hunger.

But suddenly they came upon a little house all made of gingerbread, with windows of transparent sugar.

"Saved!" cried Hogsel, and he tore off a piece of the roof and stuffed it in his mouth, while Gruntel helped herself to a window pane.

Just then an ancient crone appeared from inside the little house.

"Come in, little pigs!" she cried. "You are hungry, I can see, so I will heat up the oven." (And stick you both in it, she thought – nothing nicer than roast pork!)

So Hogsel and Gruntel went inside, and the old crone heated up the oven.

"See if it's hot enough," she said. (And then I'll push you both in, she thought.)

"We're not tall enough to see into the oven," said Hogsel, and, "You have a look," said Gruntel, and when the old crone did, they pushed her in and shut the oven door.

While she was cooking, Hogsel and Gruntel polished off all the rest of the little gingerbread house and its sugar windows too. All that was left standing was the oven, from which came a strong smell of cooking crone.

"I'm full," said Gruntel at last.

"Me too," said Hogsel.

"What about her?" said Gruntel.

"I couldn't eat another thing," said Hogsel.

So they left her to stew in her own juice.

The Princess and the Pig

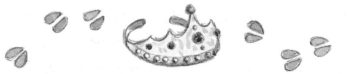

A beautiful princess was one day walking along a country road when she saw a large pig sitting on the grass verge.

Being of a kindly nature, she stopped to speak to it.

"Hullo, piggy," she said with a smile.

"Hi," said the pig. "Though actually I'm a handsome youth. I upset the local witch, with the results you can see."

"What did you say to her?" asked the princess.

"I called her a dirty smelly ugly evil old bag," said the pig. "So she put a spell on me. 'Only a kiss from a beautiful princess can change things now,' she said, and off she went, cackling with laughter."

"Oh," said the princess.

She looked at the pig doubtfully.

But then, because she was of a kindly nature, she bent down and, shutting her eyes and screwing up her courage, planted a kiss on the end of the pig's rubbery snout.

Immediately the princess also turned into a pig.

The Queen's Pig

Said a pig to his mother, "I'm terribly keen
To travel to London to talk to the Queen.
I need to consult her, while paying a visit,
About my idea." Said his mother, "What is it?"
"It's this," said the piglet. "As I understand,
Men, women and children all over the land
Eat bits of the pig as a part of their diet."
"You're right," said his mother. "I cannot
  deny it."
"Suppose," said the piglet, "The Queen should
  proclaim
With all the authority due to her name
That anyone eating a pig was a sinner?
Why, nobody ever would have us for dinner
Or breakfast or luncheon or afternoon tea,
If it was forbidden by Royal Decree."
"You've got to be joking, my boy. Pull the other
One – it's got the bells on it," snorted his mother.

"You talk to the Queen? How d'you get to
   her? Fly?"
"Pigs can't," said her son, "but I'm going.
   Goodbye."
And happily humming a popular ditty
Set off on the road to the capital city.

★

Arriving in London, his trotters quite sore
From pounding the shoulder along the M4,
Amazed at the number of streets and the thunder
Of traffic, the piglet stood gaping in wonder,
Till after a while a policeman drew near
And said to the runaway, "What's all this 'ere?"
In tones that were friendly and quite
    without malice.
"Which way," said the piglet, "to
    Buckingham Palace?"
"I'll tell you, me lad," the policeman replied,
"But don't you go thinking they'll let you inside.
'Er Majesty's usual orders, of course, is
'No animals in 'ere but corgis and 'orses'."

★

Indeed, when the piglet walked into the yard,
The sentry on duty bawled, "Turn out the guard!"
And guardsmen came rushing from every quarter
Intent, so it seemed to the piglet, on slaughter.
At sight of the soldiers he took to his heels
And ran through their legs with a volley of
   squeals.
Straight in through the door of the Palace
   he scurried
And up a great carpeted staircase he hurried.
Through corridors, passages, hallways he tore

Until by good fortune he chanced on a door
On which was a notice. QUEEN ONLY, it stated.
I've found her at last, thought the piglet, elated,
And then – nothing venture, they say,
   nothing win –

He knocked on the door and a voice said,
   "Come in."
Obeying this order, he found the Queen sitting
Surrounded by corgis and doing some knitting.
The corgis all barked and the Queen said,
   "Tut! Tut!
Shut up, do you hear me?" and up they all shut.
"And now," said the Queen, "what's the
   matter, young shaver?"
"I've come," said the piglet, "to ask you a favour,
Your Majesty, if you'll allow me to speak."
"A piglet addressing a Queen! What a cheek!"
The Monarch replied, but she couldn't
   help smiling –
The piglet was looking so cute and beguiling.
"Go on. Ask your favour then. What's all the
   fuss?"
"Please, Ma'am," said the piglet, "please
   stop eating us."

"What's that?" said the Queen. "If we're
   not much mistaken,
"You're asking us if we will stop eating bacon

And sausage and ham and pigs' trotters
    and pork –
Prince Philip will think that is no way to talk,
He loves eating crackling and so do the others,
My sister, my mummy, and Charles and
    his brothers.
Is that what you're asking?" The piglet
    said, "Yes.

That's just the idea that I came to express.
I truly and earnestly hope to inveigle
Your Majesty into declaring illegal
The eating of pig-meat of every sort.
It's only the Queen that can do it, I thought.
If she should forbid it, then no one would
    risk it."
"I must say," the Queen said, "you do take
    the biscuit!
I certainly see you'd be filled with relief
If I were to legislate 'Let them eat beef'
Or chicken or turkey or mutton or lamb
But never pork sausages, bacon or ham.
For you and your lot that would be the solution.
For me, it would certainly mean revolution!
They'd take off my crown and, quite likely,
    my head.
I'd sooner eat pig-meat than finish up dead."

So glum did the piglet appear when she'd
    spoken –
His mission a failure, his heart all but broken –
That quickly the Queen added, "Do stay to tea –

It's only the corgis and Philip and me –
And how would you like (for with you I've
    no quarrel)
To live out the rest of your days at Balmoral?"
And that is the tale of the piglet that met
The Queen and remained as Her Majesty's pet.

Though in his crusade for his kind he was beaten,
By Royal Decree he could never be eaten
But lived his long life in a fine Scottish sty –
The apple of good Queen Elizabeth's eye.

Little Red Riding Pig

Little Red Riding Pig set out one day to visit her grandmother.

She was called Little Red Riding Pig because she was small, of a ginger colour, and always rode about on her BMX bike.

Cycling through a forest glade, she met a wolf.

"Hold it right there, baby," said the wolf.

Little Red Riding Pig held it.

"Where you headin'?" said the wolf.

"To visit my grandmother," replied Little Red Riding Pig.

The wolf thought quickly. Not a lot of meat on this piglet, he said to himself, but the granny – now she might make a square meal.

"Your granny kinda fat?" he asked in a casual way.

"Oh yes!" said Little Red Riding Pig.
"She's very fat."

"Sure like to meet her," said the wolf.
"She live around here some place?"

"Oh yes!" said Little Red Riding Pig,
and she told the wolf how to get to her
grandmother's house, and away he went.

When he arrived, he knocked on the door
and a voice called, "Come in, my dear," so
he did.

There, lying in bed, was the fattest pig
the wolf had ever seen.

"Goodness me!" said the pig. "I thought

you were my little granddaughter."

" 'Fraid not, ma'am," said the wolf.

"But I see now," said Little Red Riding Pig's grandmother, "that you are in fact a handsome stranger. What big ears you have!"

All the better to hear you with, thought the wolf, but he kept his mouth shut.

"And what big eyes you have!"

All the better to see you with, thought the wolf, but he said nothing, merely opening his jaws in a kind of silent laugh.

"And what big teeth you have!" said the fat pig, and before the wolf could think about that, she went on, "Which reminds me, I have the toothache. I should be so grateful if you could look and see which tooth is causing the trouble."

"Why, sure, ma'am," said the wolf, and he approached the bed, dribbling slightly at the thought of the feast in store.

The fat pig opened her mouth wide, and the wolf bent his head to look into it.

★

Not long afterwards Little Red Riding Pig came pedalling up on her BMX. Usually, when she knocked on the door, her grandmother would call, "Come in, my dear," but now all she heard was a grunt.

She opened the door.

Her grandmother looked even fatter than usual. And there was something else odd about her.

"Why, Granny," cried Little Red Riding Pig in amazement, "you have grown a long grey beard!"

But it was only the wolf's tail, still sticking out of her grandmother's mouth.

Goldipig and the Three Bears

Goldipig was a very inquisitive little swine, always poking her snout into other people's business.

Rooting about in the forest one day, she came upon a house among the trees. "I wonder who lives there?" said Goldipig, and when she had called "Hullo!" and no one had answered, she pushed open the door and went in.

The first thing she saw was a table with three chairs around it, one big, one ordinary-sized, one little, and on the table, in front of each chair, was a bowl of porridge, one big, one ordinary-sized, one little.

Goldipig scoffed the lot.

Then, nosy as ever, she trotted upstairs. There in a bedroom were three beds, one

big, one ordinary-sized, one little.

"I'll have a nap," said Goldipig, feeling rather full.

She tried each bed in turn. The first was too little, the second too ordinary, but the third, the big bed, was just right, so Goldipig snuggled down and went to sleep.

Shortly afterwards the owners of the house returned. They had been taking a walk to work up an appetite for breakfast. They were in fact three bears, one big, one ordinary-sized, one little.

"Who's been sitting on our chairs?" said the little bear.

"And where's our porridge gone?" said the ordinary-sized bear.

"And who," said the big bear, listening carefully, "is that snoring upstairs?"

Very quietly the three bears climbed to the bedroom and looked in and saw Goldipig.

"She's messed up all our beds," said the little bear.

"After eating all our porridge," said the ordinary-sized bear.

"And so," said the big bear, "we'll jolly well eat her."

At that, Goldipig let out an enormous squeal, dashed past the bears and rushed downstairs and away. So you can see the three of them got neither porridge nor ham for their breakfast!

The Owl and the Pussy-cat

You all know that the Owl and the Pussy-cat went to sea in a beautiful pea-green boat. But do you remember the Piggy-wig they met in a wood with a ring at the end of his nose? And do you ever wonder what he did with the shilling that they gave him? Well, read on . . .

Said the Piggy, "I Will"

"At last," said the Piggy-wig, "I can rootle!"

Rootling in the ground with their strong snouts is something all pigs love doing, but they cannot rootle if they have rings in their noses.

"At last," said the Piggy-wig again, "I am rid of that horrid ring. And what's more, that Owl and that Pussy-cat

actually paid me for it! A whole shilling!
Though I do not know what on earth to do
with it. But talking of earth gives me an
idea," and he dug a little hole with his
snout and buried the shilling in a safe
place, under the Bong-tree. Then off he
went all around the wood, rootling and
rootling to his heart's content.

He had turned up all sorts of nice things
– bulbs and roots and beetles – when

suddenly his snout struck upon something hard. It was a large spoon, whose handle had been bent at right angles to its bowl by the force of the pig's rootling.

At that moment the Turkey who lives on the hill came strutting by.

"That spoon won't be much use to you at the wedding-feast," he said.

"I haven't been asked," said the pig.

"Pity," said the turkey. "They're having mince. And slices of quince."

The pig licked his lips.

"I could get you an invite," said the turkey.

"Could you?" said the pig eagerly.

"At a price."

"How much?"

"One shilling."

"Done!" said the pig, and he rushed back
to the Bong-tree and dug up his shilling
and gave it to the turkey.

Next day the Owl and the Pussy-cat
were married by the Turkey who lives on

the hill. All the invited guests (including the pig) were there, and all had brought wedding presents (except the pig).

"What can I give them?" he whispered anxiously to the turkey, who sniggered and replied, "Give 'em that old spoon."

Quickly, for he did not want to miss the wedding-feast, the pig ran back to the wood and found the spoon.

When he returned with it, he could see that something was wrong. The Pussy-cat was in tears, the Owl was trying to comfort her, and the guests were tut-tutting and dear-dearing among themselves.

"All ruined!" cried the Pussy-cat. "All wasted!"

"O lovely Pussy!" said the Owl. "Whatever's the matter?"

"Mince!" cried the Pussy-cat. "And slices of quince! There's only one possible way to eat them and that we cannot do!"

At this moment the Piggy-wig pushed his way through the crowd of guests, and dropped before the unhappy couple the large spoon with the right-angled handle.

"Hope you'll be very happy," he said gruffly.

"O Piggy-wig!" cried the Pussy-cat, drying her tears. "Now we most certainly shall be! Your wedding present is the one thing that we needed, the one thing without which it is not possible to dine on mince, and slices of quince!"

"O Pussy my love!" said the Owl, looking in puzzlement at the Piggy-wig's present. "What is it?"

"You elegant fowl!" laughed the Pussy-cat joyfully. "It's a runcible spoon!"

PUFFIN BOOKS

Published by the Penguin Group
Penguin Books Ltd, 27 Wrights Lane, London W8 5TZ, England
Penguin Putnam Inc., 375 Hudson Street, New York, New York 10014, USA
Penguin Books Australia Ltd, Ringwood, Victoria, Australia
Penguin Books Canada Ltd, 10 Alcorn Avenue, Toronto, Ontario, Canada M4V 3B2
Penguin Books (NZ) Ltd, Private Bag 102902, NSMC, Auckland, New Zealand

Penguin Books Ltd, Registered Offices: Harmondsworth, Middlesex, England

First published in *Dick King-Smith's Triffic Pig Book* by Victor Gollancz Ltd 1991
Hogsel and Gruntel published in Gollancz Children's Paperbacks 1996
Published in Puffin Books 1998
7 9 10 8 6

Text copyright © Foxbusters Ltd, 1991
Illustrations copyright © Liz Graham-Yooll, 1996
All rights reserved

The moral right of the author and illustrator has been asserted

Printed in Hong Kong by Wing King Tong

British Library Cataloguing in Publication Data
A CIP catalogue record for this book is available from the British Library

ISBN 0–140–38898–2